DOUWLINA

A Rhino's Story

bright sky press

HOUSTON, TEXAS

bright sky press
HOUSTON, TEXAS

2365 Rice Blvd., Suite 202
Houston, Texas 77005

Library of Congress Cataloging-in-Publication Data

Borgeson, Grace, 1963-
Douwlina : a rhino's story / Grace Borgeson.
p. cm.
ISBN 978-1-936474-63-9
1. Rhinoceroses—Conservation—South Africa—Juvenile literature.
2. Wildlife rescue—South Africa—Juvenile literature. 3. Poaching—South Africa—Juvenile literature. 4. Orphaned
animals—South Africa—Juvenile literature.
5. Hoedspruit Endangered Species Centre—Juvenile literature. I. Title.

QL737.U63B67 2012
599.66'80968—dc23   2012022190

10   9   8   7   6   5   4   3   2   1

Photographs generously contributed by Mrs. Lente Roode,
Johan and Annales, Joseph Borgeson and Grace Borgeson
Photo on page 10 compliments of Hoedspruit Endangered Species Centre

Editorial Direction, Lucy Herring Chambers
Creative Direction, Ellen Peeples Cregan
Design, Marla Garcia

Printed in Canada through Friesens

For all who love Douwlina
and have sacrificed
to give her the chance to live

and especially to
Johan, Annales and their family
and Daniel Ma-Africa Mosia
who strive each day to provide Douwlina with
a protected and healthy environment.

May the Lord continue to bless
the work of your hands and
grant you the privilege of sharing
Douwlina's story of victory and love.

Love never fails

- 1 CORINTHIANS 13:8 -

There are two kinds of stories in the world. There are those that have sad endings and those that have happy endings.

Douwlina's story has a happy ending.

Douwlina is a White Rhinoceros.

Did you know that there are two kinds of rhinoceros in Africa?

There are Black Rhinos and White Rhinos. These names have nothing to do with color. For the most part, Black and White Rhinos look alike, **but here are a few differences.**

If you look at a Black Rhino's mouth, you will see a pointed upper lip that turns down. **Black Rhinos** use this lip to grab the leaves and branches that they eat. They are **called browsers.**

White Rhinos' mouths are wide and flat, handy for gathering brush and grass from the ground. **White Rhinos** are **called grazers.**

WHITE RHINO

Another way you can tell the difference is by looking at the mothers and babies.
White Rhino babies, called calves, **run in front of their mothers.**
Black Rhino calves run behind their moms.
Douwlina is a White Rhino who lives in South Africa.

BLACK RHINO

Let me tell you her story.

Douwlina's story did not begin happily. The day she was born, her mother was killed by poachers. Poachers are people who kill animals illegally using traps, poison or firearms. They are not hunters. **Poaching and hunting are different.**

Hunting is legal. Hunters buy licenses, and the money from the licenses is used to support wildlife organizations. These groups make sure game populations are strong and healthy.

Animals who don't have a safe place to live are **in danger of becoming extinct.** They cannot have enough babies for their species—their type of animal—to survive.

The world once had many rhinos, all over Africa and Asia. Now, **poachers are killing rhinos so fast** that soon our planet may have **no more rhinos.** Why would people do such a terrible thing as poaching?

Some people say that **the horn of a rhino has special powers** of healing.

Scientists say that **rhino horns are just horns.** But because these people believe that rhino horns have power, they want one. And they pay the poachers lots of money to get them.

Douwlina's mother was **killed for her horn.**

DOUWLINA

▶ *Zebras and impalas live peacefully near rhinos in South Africa.*

Little Douwlina was rescued and then cared for by people working at the Hoedspruit Endangered Species Centre in South Africa. She was the youngest rhino they had ever saved. She could not sleep alone, so the kind people at the Centre took turns sleeping with her and gave her a real lamb to be her friend and care for her.

When she was strong enough, Douwlina left the Centre and went to live with a family. Annales and Johan took her to live on their farm.

When she arrived at her new home, she had never lived in the wild.

At the Centre, she only knew the love and care of humans. Now Annales and Johan and their children Annelie, Martina and Marthinus loved and cared for her. They wanted so much for her to be able to return to the wild and live happily with other rhinos.

No one knew if Douwlina would ever **choose to live** with her **own species.**

▶ *A vervet monkey sounds an alarm from high in a tree.*

Douwlina grew quickly, and she enjoyed the company of people very much. Imagine a full-grown rhinoceros thinking that she is a person!

One afternoon, Douwlina decided to join Annales and Johan in their farmhouse. She walked right onto the porch and simply **stuck her head through the closed window.** Glass shattered everywhere. Luckily, no one was harmed but you can see the difficulties that are presented when **a rhino wants to come in for a visit.**

Douwlina also liked to jog. Often Annales would go out for a run, and Douwlina would join her. **Imagine a full grown White Rhino running by your side as you jog down your street!**

ANNALES

Visitors to the farm would find Douwlina at the gate to greet them. Because she preferred the company of people, Douwlina would often sit at the front gate with the security guards. Before anyone could enter, they would have to wait for Douwlina to move out of the way. Her big body would completely block the road!

The first time I met Douwlina, she came strolling down the road towards my car. I was not sure what to think. Was she coming in peace or would she try to push the car out of her way?

JOHAN

Much to my surprise, she walked right up to my window, leaned her heavy body against the side of the car door and waited for me to scratch her back. A full grown rhino who wants to rub against a car also has the strength to dent a car, and I was worried. She did not dent my car that day, but in her eagerness to visit with people, she has left a number of scratches and dents on other vehicles.

GRACE

15

Since Douwlina did not grow up in the wild, she needed to be taught how to do a number of things that other rhinos naturally learn from their mothers. These skills help little rhinos take care of themselves when they are adults. Without a mother to teach her, Douwlina didn't even know how to take a mud bath. Mud baths are very important for rhinos, because the dried mud protects their skin from ticks and insects.

Someone would have to teach Douwlina this skill. Marthinus volunteered to be her instructor, and now Douwlina is able to bathe herself. Can you imagine rolling around in the mud with a young rhino as your student?

Douwlina continued to surprise and entertain everyone on the farm, but the question still remained:

Would Douwlina ever choose to live in the wild with the other rhinos?

MARTHINUS

▶ *Other species also need our protection, including the enormous African elephant.*

Douwlina had always been aware that two other rhinos lived on the farm. The male is named Roger; and the female, Tina.

DANIEL

Tina and Roger would have accepted Douwlina as part of their group with no problems, but Douwlina had always chosen the company of people.

Day after day, Daniel, the farm manager, **walked Douwlina** to the back of the farm to **spend time** with the **other two rhinos.** Day after day, **Douwlina would return** with him **to the house.** The family worried about her, and they talked about ways to make her comfortable with her own kind. Nothing they did worked. **Douwlina was not ready to live with other rhinos.**

One morning, Daniel went out to take her to visit Tina and Roger. **Douwlina was gone.** Daniel looked all over the farm for her, getting more and more worried. And then **he found her.** She had made the choice on her own.

Douwlina was back in the wild with her own species.

▶ *The tallest animal in the world, the giraffe, also lives in South Africa.*

Today, thanks to the love and care of her human friends, Douwlina lives with the other rhinos. **Her story has a happy ending.** Douwlina's story reminds us that we have a choice about how we treat the animals who live with us on our planet. It is **our responsibility** to be **good stewards of the animals** and the land we all share.

21

Just as I have shared Douwlina's story with you, you can share it with others. If all the people who care about rhinos don't speak up and stop the poaching, sadly, there will be no more rhinos. They will become extinct.

When we tell others about the animals we care for, we raise awareness. When more people understand the dangers that these species face, more people who have the ability to make change choose to get involved with their workers and supplies.

Douwlina's story reminds us

that a tragic beginning does not have to end in sorrow. At the time of her birth, **only God knew if she would live and one day thrive.** The goodness of God worked through the love and kindness of people **caring for His little rhino.**

23

When I first heard Douwlina's story,

I was sad that I couldn't do anything to help her and the other rhinos. Then I realized that what I needed to do was **share her story with others.** Together we can make sure that **all rhinos have a happy ending** to their story.

I have told Douwlina's story to people around the world. I told my son Joseph about her, and he drew these pictures.

I hope you will share Douwlina's story with others. You will be raising awareness, and **your voice will join with others** who rescue and support wildlife. When enough people know and care about rhinos like Douwlina, we can **finally stop the poaching.**

Since I met Douwlina, I have learned many facts about rhinos. Did you know:

- There are 5 species of rhino, 2 African and 3 Asian.
- Both African rhino species have two horns.
- Rhinos in their natural habitat live between 35 and 40 years.
- All rhinos have three toes on each foot.
- The word rhinoceros is of Greek origin from the word *rhino*, meaning "nose" and the word *ceros*, meaning "horn."
- An adult Black Rhino weighs between 2000 and 3000 pounds.
- An adult White Rhino weighs between 4000 and 5500 pounds.
- Rhinos can hear and smell very well but have poor eyesight.
- Both African rhino species can run at a top speed of 28 miles per hour.
- A female rhino is pregnant between 14 and 18 months.
- Calves nurse for a year but can eat vegetation one week after birth.
- Many rhinos get their horns cut to make them less attractive to poachers. Because a rhino's horn is like our fingernails, it will grow back over time. You might notice that in some of Douwlina's photos she has her horn cut.

▶ *One of Africa's ancient trees, the baobab is known as the "tree of life" because it holds precious water.*

ACKNOWLEDGEMENTS

It would not be possible for me to share Douwlina's story without the help of these friends and organizations. In addition to telling me the stories of Douwlina's life before I met her, they shared pictures, information and enthusiasm. Their dedication to helping Douwlina and other rhinos has been truly inspirational to me. I offer my gratitude to:

- Mrs. Lente Roode and the Hoedspruit Wildlife Rehabilitation Centre,
- Johan, Annales and their children,
- Sarel of Arcon Media for creating our book proposal,
- Dira for creative coordination,
- Joseph Borgeson for illustrations,
- Rose White from the Timbavati Game Reserve for editing and content,
- Henk Shmidt of Arcon Africa Architects who made it possible for me to live on the farm,
- Lucy, Ellen and Marla at Bright Sky Press for all their hard work, patience and faithfulness,
- my dear friend, Monica, for sacrificially standing by me and supporting me at all times,
- my beloved husband, Shawn, whose love and faithfulness is unwavering, and my beautiful children — Cole, Joseph and Blake — who remind me daily that children are truly a blessing from the Lord,
- my partners at Dira — Alex, Christy and Lauren — for their continual love, support and sacrifice to create this book,
- and special thanks to Daniel Ma-Africa Mosia, the General Manager of the farm, who patiently and faithfully walked with Douwlina until she was ready to join her own.

I give thanks to my heavenly Father, in Jesus' name, for giving me the gift of sharing Douwlina's story.

A portion of the profits from this book will go to organizations dedicated to rescuing and raising the orphans of poached female rhinos and to the care and nurture of other orphaned or wounded wildlife.